Salty Splashes

COLLECTION™

Salty Splashes

COLLECTION™

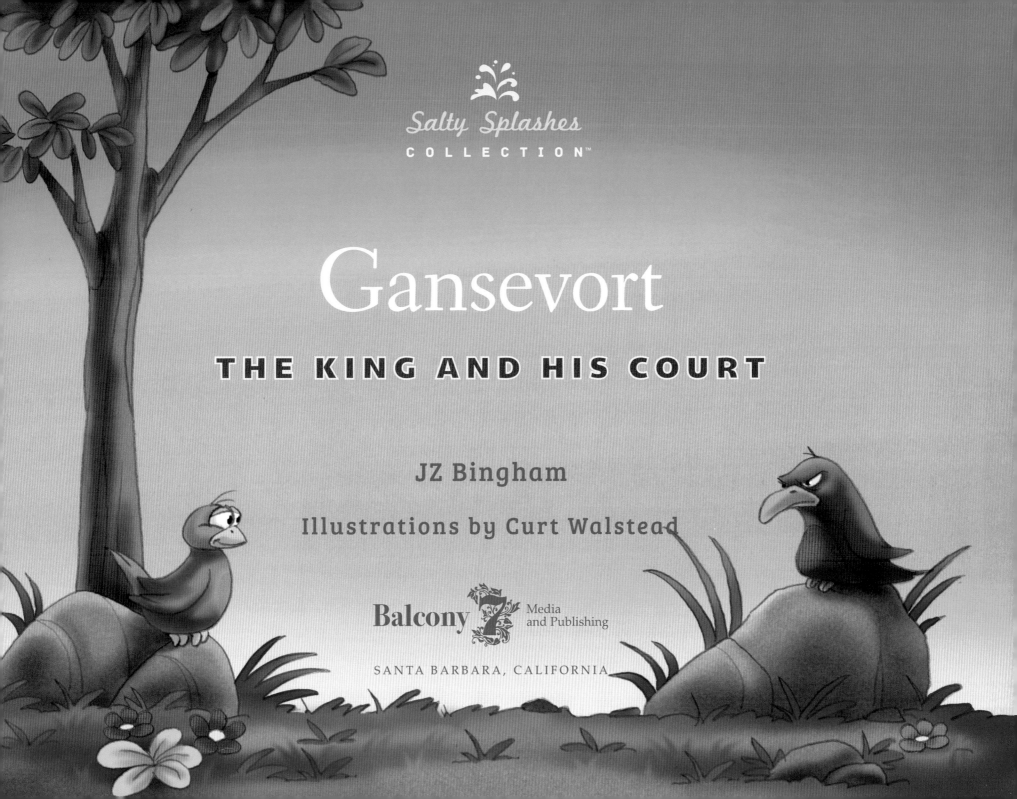

Salty Splashes COLLECTION™

Gansevort

THE KING AND HIS COURT

JZ Bingham

Illustrations by Curt Walstead

Balcony 7 Media and Publishing

SANTA BARBARA, CALIFORNIA

Printed in the United States of America

ISBN: 978-0-9855453-8-3
Library of Congress Control Number: 2012918576

Additional copies of this book, including bulk orders, are
available at www.balcony7.com

Published by Balcony 7 Media and Publishing LLC
133 East De La Guerra St., #177
Santa Barbara, CA 93101
(805) 679-1821
info@balcony7.com
www.balcony7.com

Printed by Lehigh Phoenix

Book Design and Production by DesignForBooks.com
Art Direction, Character and Storyboard Development: Balcony 7 Studios
Cover Art and Interior Illustrations: Curt Walstead

To Samira, yet again . . .
Maybe not a Queen,
but certainly my little Princess.

Salty Splashes
C O L L E C T I O N™

www.saltysplashes.com

Also by J.Z. Bingham

Dreamy Drums, Trouble in Paradise

Isle of Mystery, Eyes of the King

A Salty Splashes Collection™

Introduction

Welcome to the *Salty Splashes Collection*™, a world of illustrated fiction for children. *Salty Splashes* tales are told in playful rhymes which are lots of fun to read by kids, as well as adults. Meet our lovable cartoon cast: a precocious bunch who seem to find trouble wherever they go; but they always stick together and learn important lessons along the way. You can meet new characters in every story and join in their antics and adventure. *Salty Splashes* books are in a numbered series but can be enjoyed in any order.

Children of all ages will love these stories because the colorful, detailed illustrations describe every scene and make learning words easier and more exciting.

A balance of easy and more difficult words will help kids expand their vocabulary. Story time is more fun with our mix of narrative and character dialogue because kids can engage in role play, all in rhyme.

Gansevort is the third book in the *Salty Splashes Collection*™. The cast has made a new friend on the island, who warns them of the ornery King and his Court. The storyboard designs of Balcony 7 Studios, combined with the hand-drawn illustrations of Curt Walstead, help bring the characters and their cartoon world to life. With every turn of the page, and with every twist in the story, you will almost hear their voices come to life as well. Stay tuned . . . Soon, you actually will . . .

~ J.Z. Bingham

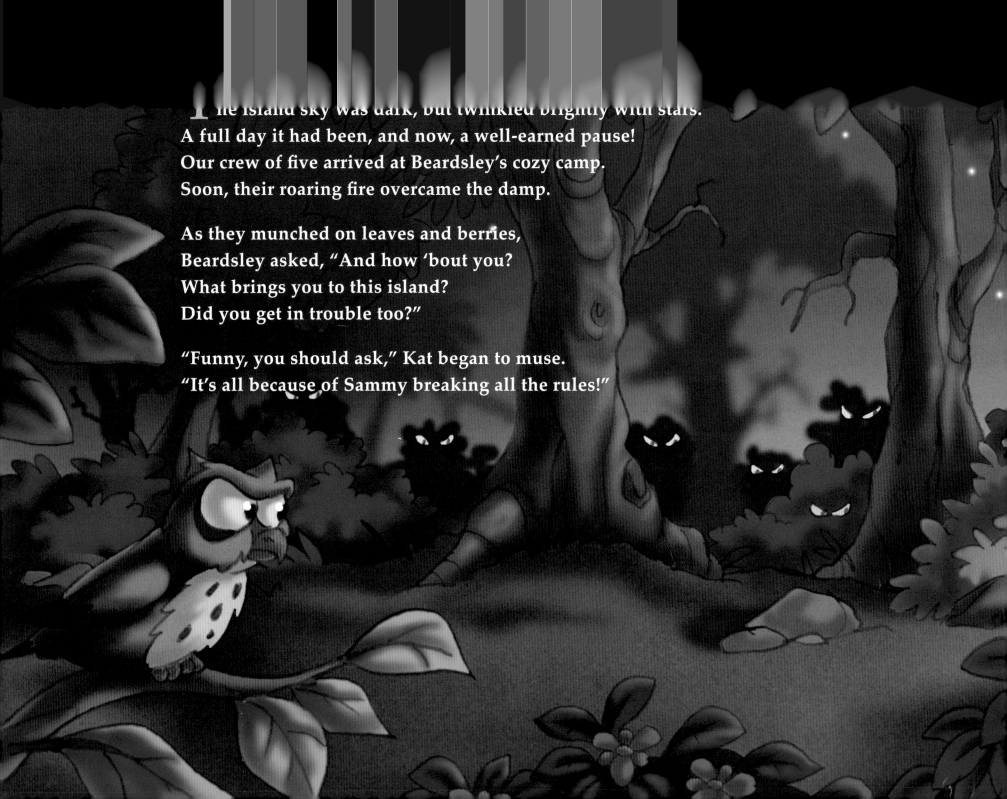

The island sky was dark, but twinkled brightly with stars.
A full day it had been, and now, a well-earned pause!
Our crew of five arrived at Beardsley's cozy camp.
Soon, their roaring fire overcame the damp.

As they munched on leaves and berries,
Beardsley asked, "And how 'bout you?
What brings you to this island?
Did you get in trouble too?"

"Funny, you should ask," Kat began to muse.
"It's all because of Sammy breaking all the rules!"

"That's not fair!" Sammy cried out, angrily.
"I didn't know the boat would take us out to sea!"

Beardsley had a laugh, "All that spunk is nice to see!
It'll serve you well here, if you want to stay free . . ."

"What's THAT supposed to mean?" Kat asked curiously.

"Oh, just that the forces here are not that friendly . . .
I'm afraid that your stay here will have to be short;
This island is controlled by King Gansevort."

"A King?" Sammy joked, "Like with a robe and a crown?"

"Yes, a KING, not a JOKE. He ties his visitors down!"

"Ties them down!" Melrose gulped, "Why? What's his beef?"

"Exactly, fuzzy friend! HE's the beef! The Beef CHIEF!
He's a steer, left behind from the old cattle ranch.
If his bully foxes find you, you'll be tied down to a branch!"

As they listened to his words, the dire message sunk in:
As soon as morning came, they'd have to sail again!

"Our boat!" Kat cried out, "We have to get it back!"

"In the morning, we'll go look to see that it's intact.
In the meantime," Beardsley yawned, "Let's all get some rest.
Tomorrow will be sure to put you to the test!"

Kat slept in Beardsley's cave while he slept outside.
Sammy and the others curled around the fireside.

The stars twinkled brightly through the canopy of trees.
The leaves were gently rustling in the soft ocean breeze.
The campfire spilled its warmth toward where they lay,
Like a blanket of sweet dreams to melt away the day.

The morning sun was shining bright as Kat awoke.
She smiled and watched Beardsley give the fire a poke.
She looked around the camp, "Where'd everyone go?"
Beardsley slowly turned, his eyes heavy, voice low.

"You see this 'G' branded on this tree?
It stands for 'Gansevort,' a great ranch it used to be . . .
But that was long ago; now, it's the name of the King.
He made the island private; there's No Trespassing . . .
His tribe of foxes troll the island night and day,
To look for any visitors who stray his way . . .
The foxes brand the 'G' to mark what they've done:
In the middle of the night, they took them, one by one . . ."

Kat's pretty green eyes shed but one lone tear.
Then her mouth began to twist into a devilish sneer.
"Beardsley," she whispered, "now you listen to me . . .
You have to take me to them, immediately . . .
I'm not leaving from this island, until they're free!"
To make her point clear, she scratched her nails over the "G!"

Beardsley, taken aback by the force of her attack,
Could see every single hair standing up on her back.

"Foxes, so you say? Well, I can play their game!"
She smeared red berries on her face, "A new face! A new name!"

"What, may I ask, are you planning to do?
Don't you think those foxes will be on to you?"

"They don't know I'm here! A cat like me they've never seen!
I plan on marching in, and acting TOUGH and MEAN!
I'll DEMAND to see their King, and make a GREAT BIG SCENE!
They'll bow down before my eyes! They'll think that I'm their QUEEN!"

Beardsley's jaw dropped; he didn't know what to say.
But then it dawned on him, there might be no other way.

"You can't do this all alone; no, I can't have that . . ."
Then he rolled himself in soot, becoming a big black cat!
"A black panther for the Queen, to make her grand entrance!"

Kat laughed, "You look so MEAN! We just might have a chance!"

"We have no other choice . . . but before we try,
I think we should send smoke signals into the sky.
Someone's bound to see; and, we might get lucky . . .
Some help just might arrive in time to rescue those three."

Their plan in place, they set out to perform their roles:
A regal Queen; a panther, mean; big puffs of smoke soon rose.
Quietly, they marched toward the camp of the King.
The stage, they knew, was set, for an epic happening.

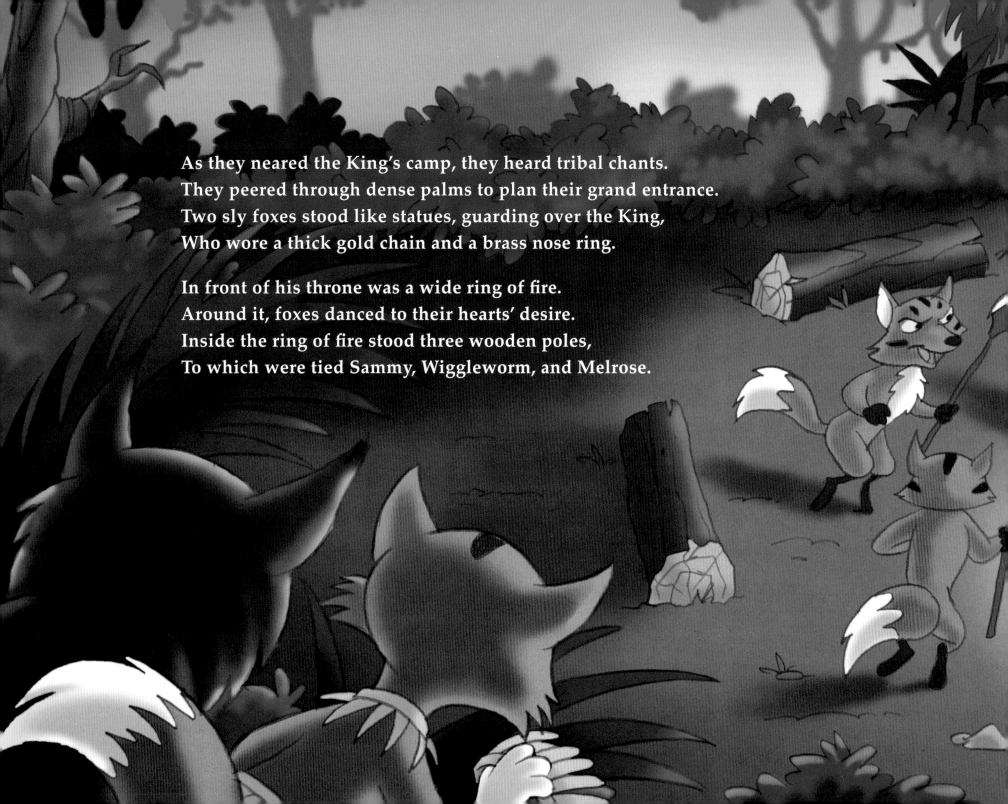

As they neared the King's camp, they heard tribal chants.
They peered through dense palms to plan their grand entrance.
Two sly foxes stood like statues, guarding over the King,
Who wore a thick gold chain and a brass nose ring.

In front of his throne was a wide ring of fire.
Around it, foxes danced to their hearts' desire.
Inside the ring of fire stood three wooden poles,
To which were tied Sammy, Wiggleworm, and Melrose.

The King raised his hoof and the foxes froze.
From his throne, his massive frame very slowly rose.

The Fox Chief kneeled before him, "Hail! Your Majesty!
Your wish is my command! Shall I sentence these three?"

"Yes! It is time!" Gansevort commanded.

His voice was deep and dark; respect, it demanded.
He moved his hefty frame toward the center of the ring.
Sammy bravely met the coal-black eyes of the King.

Beardsley looked at Kat. She smiled back confidently,
"Beardsley, how's about we crash this stupid party?"

"Your wish is my command, your Majesty!"
He boldly stepped ahead, brushing past the palm tree.

All eyes turned their way, and they stared in awe.
"Her Majesty, the Queen! Bow down! One and all!"
Beardsley's booming voice took them by surprise.
The foxes cowered down before their very eyes!

Gansevort, confused, turned with mouth opened wide.
Kat walked toward him prettily, with a Queenly stride.
Beardsley followed closely, looking fierce and mean.
They stopped before the King; what a regal scene!

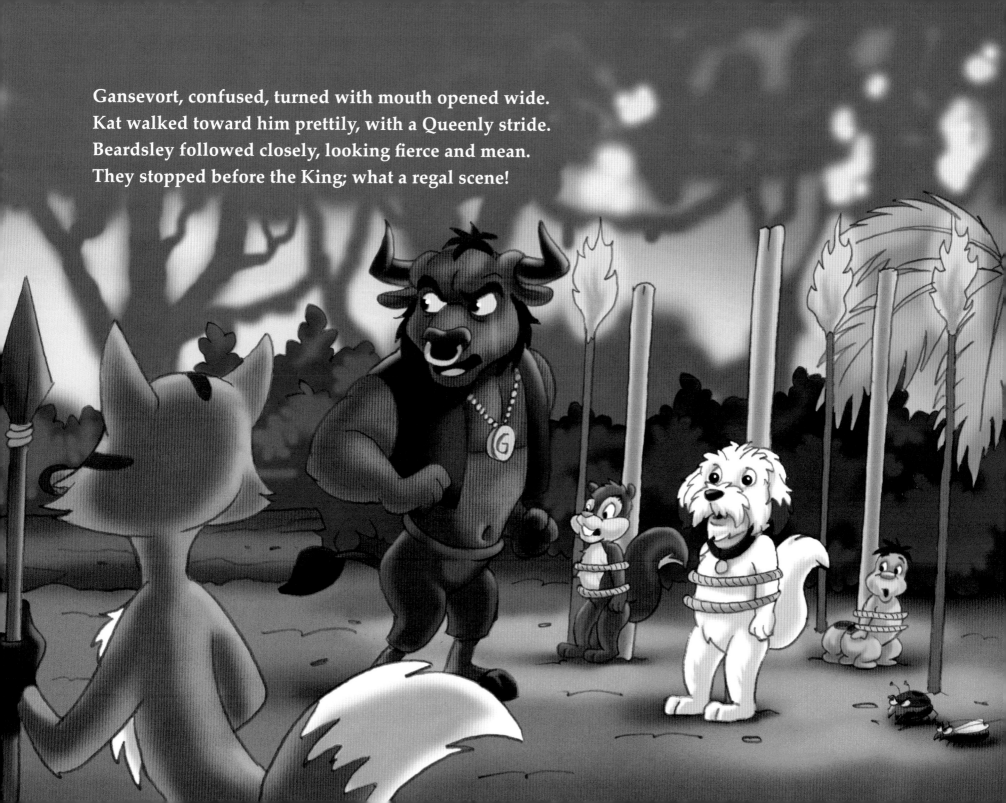

Kat held her head high as she met the King's eye.
Her stare was bold, yet sweet, and it would not die.
Gansevort looked down into these dark green pools.
And soon his tone softened as he bought her ruse.

"Your Highness!" the King bowed. "Welcome to Gansevort.
I am the King, and this, my humble court!"

"I thank your Majesty for his kind welcome.
I am Queen Samira; this, my consort, Griscome.
The storm steered us off course, and brought us to your shore.
We need one night to rest before we sail once more."

The King softened his tone and gestured toward his throne.
"It was a frightful storm. Now you are safe in my home.
We are honored to include you in our feast tonight.
I am sure you have arrived with an appetite!"

"Yes, indeed," the Queen replied as she took her seat.
"Your kindness shall be repaid." She was short and sweet.

The three prisoners looked on as this scene played out.
They were stunned but now had hope to replace their doubt.
As they watched, they saw Kat's eyes quickly scan the sky;
Then she raised her paw to point, and stood up to cry,

"Your Majesty, a FIRE! A sign of danger in store!
You must see to this now and protect your shore!"

Gansevort stood and glared up at the smoke.
"What's this?" his anger rising, as he loudly spoke.
"Lupus! Take your scouts! Report back to me at once!"
While the foxes dumbly stared, the King was losing patience.

"Quickly, I say! You silly fools! Make haste!"
Gansevort spit out these words with great distaste.

"Please excuse me Queen; I must attend to this.
You are safe with my guards; a fire is dangerous!"

"Yes, indeed, be on your way . . . and make us safe another day . . ."
She curtsied very sweetly as he set off on his way.

Now they were alone; just two foxes hovering.
Queen Samira slowly moved toward the fiery ring.
As she neared the prisoners, the guards became alert.
Then Beardsley made his move, wrestling them into the dirt!

Their plan was now in play; they had no time to lose.
If the King found out, they knew he'd surely blow a fuse!
Kat untied the three; Beardsley tied up the guards.
They had no time for words; they were panting hard.

Beardsley took the lead; he was no longer black.
Kat carried Melrose; Wiggleworm grabbed Sammy's back.

They raced through the woods; they needed to set sail!
But soon they heard the foxes, behind them on the trail.

Up ahead was the beach; they raced on to the sand.
The foxes starting shouting; they heard Gansevort's command,

"IMPOSTOR'S!" he bellowed. "You will NOT get away!
NO ONE fools the King and lives another day!"

They had to run faster; they could not lose hope!
One by one, they jumped aboard as Beardsley untied the rope.
As the foxes closed in, the sky turned to black.
They looked up to see a huge flock of storks attack!

The foxes were outnumbered; the storks dove down with speed.
They swooped all around; even Gansevort took heed . . .

As he tried to ward them off, Beardsley pushed the boat to sea.
A school of waiting dolphins grabbed their rope and pulled them free!
The boat was gaining speed as they caught their breath.
Their dolphin escorts pulled them toward the ocean's depth.

They hugged each other warmly, taking one last look.
The scene they left behind seemed right out of a book!
The storks were backing off; their work there was done.
The battle of Gansevort, they knew, was finally won!

"Queen Samira!" Sammy said, "What an amazing plan!"
Beardsley laughed, "Your Highness! I'm your biggest fan!"

The dolphins pulled them swiftly on their long sea cruise.
Ocean air and gentle waves lulled them into a snooze.
As they neared land again, the dolphins gave out a shout.
They pulled the boat to shore before they swam back out.

"Sammy! Wake up! Do you see what I see?"
Wiggleworm was pointing toward the shore excitedly.
They all rubbed their eyes, and to their great surprise,
Their entire neighborhood was cheering joyful cries!

Back at home, they gathered 'round for a great big cake!
Mom and Dad were so relieved after nights wide awake!
They invited Beardsley into their happy home;
From now on he no longer had to be alone.

All ears perked up as Sammy started telling the tale,
Of Gansevort, his Court, and how their boat set sail.
They talked into the night, next to a fire warm and bright.
The sounds of joyous laughter seemed to add to its light.

When the sun came up, they took a long walk on the beach.
They promised, from now on, they would stay within reach.
"Yes," they thought, "we'll stick around, and just do what we love:
Have lots of fun in the sun, and not forget what's above . . ."

Mischief and adventure don't go hand in hand.
It's not good to look for trouble. It's not bad to take a stand.
It's okay to be prepared in a far away land;
And be there for your friends, when they need a helping hand.

There was no doubt, about their bout, with danger and harm.
It made their home seem that much more welcome and warm.
As they tossed a volleyball back and forth on the sand,
You could tell they all were thinking, "Ah! Life is grand!"

Salty Splashes

C O L L E C T I O N™

Salty Splashes

C O L L E C T I O N™